WRITTEN BY TENNANT REDBANK

ILLUSTRATED BY LORI TYMINSKI

Disney · PIXAR
BRAVE

DESIGNED BY STUART SMITH

randomhouse.com/kids

ISBN: 978-0-7364-2901-6

Printed in the United
States of America

10 9 8 7 6 5 4 3

🌸 A GOLDEN BOOK · NEW YORK

A princess rises early.

A princess doesn't doodle.

A princess is patient,
cautious, and clean!

Queen Elinor had **many** rules for how
to be a princess. Merida, her daughter, hated
ALL of them. Only when she was alone did
Merida feel free.

Since Merida would be queen one day and she was old enough to marry, Queen Elinor felt it was time to find her a husband.

"Marriage?" Merida wailed.

Queen Elinor and King Fergus invited the oldest sons of three lords to compete in the royal games. The winner would marry Merida!

There was Young Macintosh,

Young
MacGuffin,

and
Wee Dingwall.

Merida did not want to marry
any of them. So she won the royal
games herself!

Queen Elinor was **furious**. Merida was angry, too. She was tired of always having to do what her mother wanted. Merida lost her temper. She **slashed** her sword through a family tapestry—right between the images of her and her mother!

Then Merida jumped onto her horse
and rode away from the castle.

When she came upon a ring of stones, she saw
a flickering blue light. More lights joined it. The
will o' the wisps were forming
a trail leading her into the woods.

Merida followed the will o' the wisps to
a woodcarver's cottage. But the woodcarver
was **really a witch!** She offered to
make one spell for Merida.

Merida wanted a spell to change her mother's mind. The Witch agreed to do it and started brewing something in her cauldron. When she was done, she gave Merida a **spell cake**.

Back at the castle, Merida brought the cake to Queen Elinor. She hoped it would make her mother change her mind about the marriage. Instead, it changed Queen Elinor into a bear!

Oh, no! What had Merida done?
Years earlier, a giant bear named Mor'du
had bitten off one of the king's legs. Now
Fergus **heard** a bear. He **sensed** a bear.

Right away, Fergus knew a bear
was in the castle!

He tracked it up the stairs,

around a corner,

and
down
a hallway.

Merida's mother was a bear. Her father was hunting her mother. Merida needed help!

Merida's little brothers led Fergus on a wild-goose chase. The queen got away! To thank her brothers, Merida said they could have any treat in the kitchen.

Uh-oh!

Merida rushed back to the
Witch's cottage. The Witch was
gone, but she had left a clue: **Fate
be changed, look inside,
mend the bond torn by
pride.** What did it mean?

In the woods, Merida and her mother learned to work together. For the first time, they enjoyed each other. At last, Merida understood the Witch's clue.

"It's the tapestry!" she cried. **"Mend the bond torn by pride"** must mean fixing the tapestry would make her mother human again!

At the castle, Fergus spotted Elinor.
He thought she was a wild bear!
"Mum, run!" shouted Merida.
Fergus and the other men chased Elinor.
Merida chased the men. Her brothers helped.
They were bears now, too. They had eaten the
spell cake!

Merida had to fix
the tapestry—**fast!**

The hunting party closed in on the bear and tied her to the ground.

Fergus raised his sword. But Merida stepped in and blocked his blow! She had saved her mother, just in time.

Suddenly Mor'du appeared.
When he turned toward Merida,
her mother broke free from her
ropes. She fought Mor'du—and
won. The evil bear was crushed
by a giant stone.

Even though the tapestry was
fixed, Elinor was still a bear.
Merida threw her arms
around her mother.
"I want you back,
Mum," she said.
"I love you."

At those words, her mother
changed back into the queen!

One day, Merida might be queen. But for now, there would be no more changes. Elinor and Merida had learned to love each other just the way they were.